One of my favorite contemporary writers, Meghan Lamb's COWARD is an astonishing, jagged work. Channeling the oozing repetition of Swans, Lamb takes apart the bildungsroman in a form so visceral and jewel-like, you lose your breath. This work of transgressive genius, riddled with sex and fire and zombie love, is thrilling to behold.

Alistair McCartney, author of *The Disintegrations*

All of Meghan Lamb's work disturbs and awes in equal measure and the apocalyptic COWARD is her strongest, strangest, and most dangerous vision yet. We are fortunate witnesses of her rise to greatness.

Robert Kloss, author of *The Genocide House*

COWARD
MEGHAN LAMB

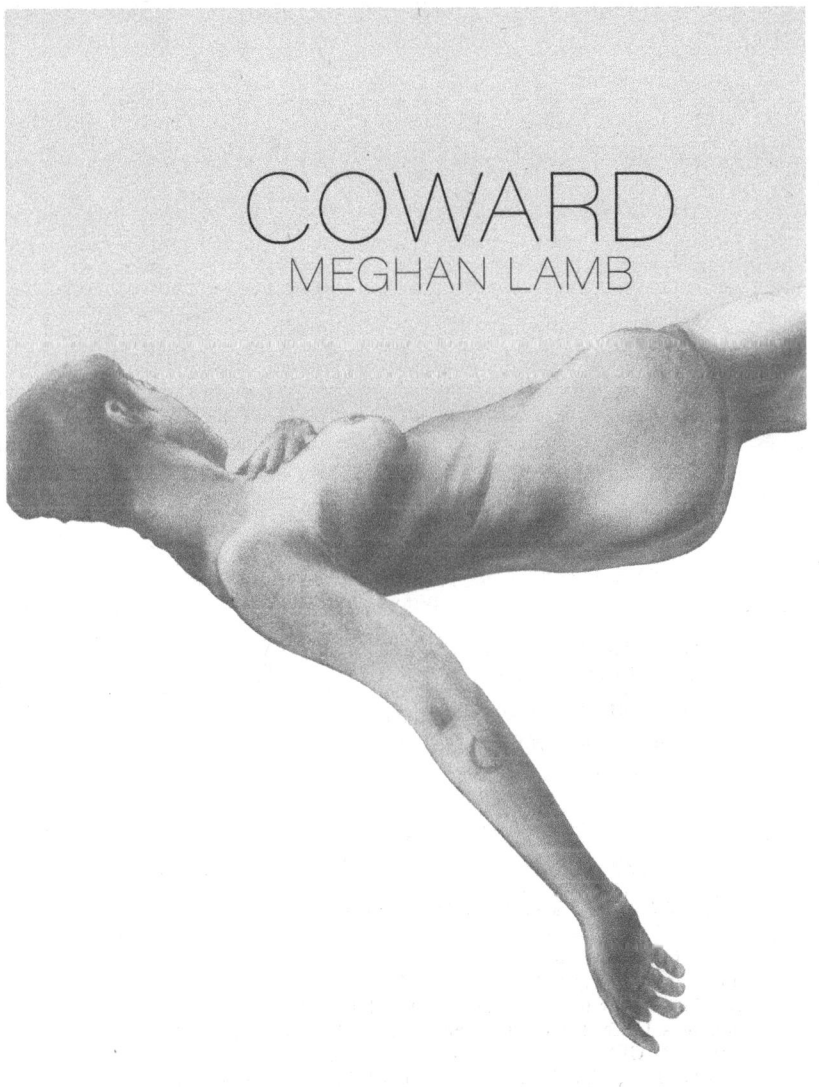

Spuyten Duyvil
New York   Paris

© 2022 Meghan Lamb
ISBN 978-1-956005-87-5
Cover art by Devon Stackonis
devonstackonis.com

Library of Congress Cataloging-in-Publication Data

Names: Lamb, Meghan, author.
Title: Coward / Meghan Lamb.
Description: New York City : Spuyten Duyvil, [2022]
Identifiers: LCCN 2022043832 | ISBN 9781956005875 (paperback)
Subjects: LCGFT: Novels.
Classification: LCC PS3612.A546226 C69 2022 | DDC 813/.6--dc23
LC record available at https://lccn.loc.gov/2022043832

The relation between what we see and what we know is never settled. Each evening we see the sun set. We know that the earth is turning away from it. Yet the knowledge, the explanation, never quite fits the sight.
—John Berger, *Ways of Seeing*

I just made you up to hurt myself.
—NiN, *Only*

I'm a coward. Put your knife in me. Put your knife in me.
—Swans, *Coward*

The sky is burning up again, the way it does each August. Like some ritual, some letting out of blood. It smells a bit of blood. Of iron, say the people from this town. Some say it smells like ore. Dark sediment. Charred skin. Meanwhile, the factories that used to make their own gray streams of sediment stand still and silent, gathering the drifts.

It always starts out with the blonde hairs of the hills, standing on edge, bristled and ready, with their bleedy scabs of brush.

The smoke begins to rise, a shimmer-hover over cracked soil, snake skins, and the ache-stretched skeleton ribs of old rail lines.

The shimmer turns to shadows.

Turns to ash.

The sky turns gray.

Then darker gray.

Then black.

The mountain forests burn. The winds rise: winds of clouds of hot debris, of smoldering destruction carried through the high plains.

Don't worry, someone tells you—for you haven't

lived through other Augusts, here. No, you do not
know. No, you are not used to this. They come in
August—yes—they burn their way through August,
and we stay in, wait, until September, but it passes,
every year.

Don't worry, they insist—for you look skeptical.
Don't worry. It is natural. It is a part of life. A cleansing
process—yes—a learning process. How to learn to
wait, to wait in hot dark rooms, looking out windows,
watching til it's safe to go outside.

—

Outside, among the shadows of the factories, the zombies gather. In their certain alleys, certain streets they've marked with piss and shit and needles and used Big Gulps that were filled with who the fuck knows what. The streets that everybody knows to not go down.

—

Inside, among the shadows of a curtained room, he lies—naked and pale—across the bare slab of his mattress.

He has it out, again. The picture that she sent him, that he knows he shouldn't keep of her—of them—Kate McClane's Perfect Breasts.

The Perfect Breasts are as they always are and always will be: rounded, pointed, and resplendent in the dim light, glowing globes of milk glass in the dim light, bowls of soft fog in the dim light, cusps of cold skin, there, but not there—here—held in his pinched hand, in the dim light.

He runs the other hand over the slick bulge of his belly, feels the pain of it digesting what he just consumed: a meal of cigarettes and condiments, whatever shit he had left in the fridge, whole jars of olives, pickles, tube of yellow mustard, a few desperate scrapings of some old congealed marmalade, and something else that tasted sweet, but now tastes sour. He feels so full and so unsatisfied. He hisses in between soft teeth. His mouth reeks of Virginia Slims and pickle juice.

The room is dry waves of this sealed warmth, but he feels wet with—what, he doesn't understand—with longing, or with loneliness? No, no, it isn't loneliness, he thinks, tapping his raw nails on the Polaroid's ridge, wishing—and not wishing—she was ever there.

The Perfect Breasts are there.

The Perfect Breasts are what he has.

The Perfect Breasts are smirking at the seething of his belly-bulge.

He knows that Kate McClane would say, *Why are you doing that? What do you want? What are you doing? What is wrong with you?*

It is this: the raw nude nerves, the under-skin itch.

It is this: the shining scabs of his scalp, the cragged lines of his chin.

And this: the sad, inevitable swelling of his cock.

And this: the weird rise of a pain that has no surface.

—

Inside, across town, in another dark room, she is lying in her nightgown—which is really just some t-shirt from her dad—some logo t-shirt from some lame team-building picnic for some big lame company that he no longer even works for. The weird cheap pseudo mesh shit that the shirt is made of makes her nipples hard, and kind of raw, and that is secretly the reason that she wears it, and she tries not to acknowledge this, but knows it—feels it—feels a bit disgusted, feeling how her skin shifts.

She looks up at the ceiling, wide-eyed, but she can't see anything. She thinks, she's waiting, but she doesn't know why. She gets the same sensation she gets when she's sick, and needs to lie still, stiff-limbed, frozen, til the waves of nausea pass.

The waiting feels like sickness, loaming in her guts. She swallows dry spit and tries to imagine it is soup. She feels her stomach stir, like helpless noodles softening. She breathes in deep, and deeper breaths, taking in slow sips of the night.

And with these slow sips, she imagines her two thirsty lungs inhaling—through the dark—the invisible hisses of Marianne Lee. Marianne Lee, who is a girl-mouth lined in light pink: little waxy smiles that smell—and likely taste—like fake strawberries. Marianne Lee, who is—by day—a girly garden full of curls and barbs, her *hmmms*, and *ahhs*, and *are you serious*-es, and—by night—oh, in that soil-dark, becomes—maybe—she thinks—this grinding, deep unearthing, low moans, like unholy bodies underground.

Marianne Lee would likely ask, *What are you wearing? Are you serious? What is that, even?* She lifts up the t-shirt edge, a bit. She takes the t-shirt off and coils it tightly in between her fingers, curls it up into a stiff embarrassed ball inside her hands.

She looks down at the curled up shirt.

Curls up into herself.

Clutching her stomach, gently rocking back and forth.

What are you doing? Are you sick, or something? Marianne Lee might say. *Are you okay? What is making you this way?*

It is this: her inner belly heat.

It is this: the scratched commingling of stubbled legs and twisting blanket yarns.

And this: the way the air takes on the stenches of her breath.

And this: the fear that no one that she wants will ever want to kiss her.

—

Outside, the air is pregnant with the smells of smoke and unwashed skin. The zombies mill around, picking their blisters. Pock hills poking out brown streaky rags of clothing. Red eyes set in red-burned faces. Gazing out into their separate, lonely pits of night. Like the whole town has become their haze, their inner rage of longing. Like the whole town has become the darkened alley. Like the whole town—all its buildings of closed windows, chambered heat—is radiating with the red pain in their eyes.

—

Kate McClane writes to him, the first time, from across the country—

A/S/L, he asks, and she replies, 19/F/Fort Wayne, IN—and he pictures what he knows of Indiana: corn fields, rusted trucks, and flat-flat-flat, vast swathes of empty land. And from this vast flat, he imagines something rising. He imagines her inside some concrete fortress, in some tower. Some old silo, hollowed out. Some shadow figure standing at the apex of a tower. Some Rapunzel of the open, empty fields.

Does she imagine him, then, likewise—23/M—looking out from his apartment, at the black clouds in the sky? Does she imagine him, then—6' 1"/thin—as handsome? Does she imagine, him, then, filling in his own imagination?

—

She learns her longing for Marianne Lee with all
her middle school girlfriends gathered in the den,
with cans of grocery store-brand diet soda—which she
offers with a downcast look at Marianne Lee, like, *ugh,
god, I'm so sorry, this is all we have.* It shouldn't be a big
deal, she knows, being with these girls, but she knows
that it is a big deal for her, thinks about her mother
running too-sharp nails through her hair, saying, *you
never see your little friends*, and, *you know, you could
be a little pretty if you tried.* They gather by the desk
her dad took from his lame job, and the shitty old
computer that he uses—now—for only playing poker.
They plug the cable in and log on, giggling about
the weird ghost-hiss-shriek-siren wail of the thing
connecting. Scroll through the chatrooms. That one!
Points Marianne Lee—who's grinning knowingly—a
room for gay men 21-30 looking to hook up.

Let's be a hot guy, says Marianne Lee. Always the
instigator, with her little nose ring, with her fishnets,
with her dyed black hair

But why the *gay* room? Her most boring friend asks, tonguing at her braces, fingering the thin chain of her silver crucifix.

Because straight guys are dumb and ugly. Marianne Lee rolls her eyes. No one will see us, obviously, so we can be anyone.

You want to be a guy? Asks her second-most boring friend.

I want to be a hot guy, clarifies Marianne Lee.

She shifts, hot-flushed there in her father's ratty roll-chair, suddenly self conscious of her boney ass, her boy-shaped kid jeans, and her boy-shaped bowl-cut hair grown out into a mop of flat-flat-flat, her insides echoing with aftershocks of everything Marianne Lee tells her to type.

22/M/California. *Male.*

Surfer body. *Body.*

Brown eyes. *Brown.*

Everyone says... *Says.*

I look like Keanu Reeves. *Look like.*

I have tattoos. *I have.*

I have a house along the beach. *I have.*

I have a swimming pool. *I have.*

I like to watch...*Watch.*

Waves at night.

23/M/NYC. You sound hot, someone writes back.

Thanks, she writes.

He sends a private message. Hey there.

She writes, hey.

She does an image search and sends a picture of Keanu Reeves, some candid shot that doesn't really look like him.

Oh fuck. You are hot, he writes.

Thanks, she writes. Can I see you?

He writes back, sorry. I don't have a lot of pictures of myself.

Marianne Lee leans in and whispers, tell him that you have a *huge*—she inhales, hesitating, swallows with a little hiss-spit—*cock.*

I have a *huge*—

Her hands are shaky, hovering above the keyboard, and she looks back at the girls around her: bored and ready to move on.

So, she signs off, and they spend two hours on some

21

dumbass game her second-most boring friend brought. Some thing where you can wander through some virtual mall, scroll through glitchy pixelated signs and storefronts, click on clothes, and drag them on some pale, sexless mannequin. They dress the mannequin in faux distressed jeans. Skirts of shreds designed to look disheveled. Midriff tops that look torn off with teeth. Thin, skin-like strips of lingerie, and coils of belts and bracelets like metallic serpents. Leather chokers that could really choke you. The strange, sick feeling: growing in her guts with each click-click, each drag, each time the trappings are removed, the naked blankness of the mannequin re-re-revealed, the shiver of the whisper—*warm*—the drizzle of the hiss-spit—*cock*—still lingering inside her.

He scrolls through rows of different shades of eyes—brown-gray, blue-gray, blue-green—and shapes of eyes—ovaline, almandine, long-lashed and heavy-lidded, sad eyes, tired eyes, salacious dark-lined bedroom eyes, cartoon eyes, angry eyes, unfocused eyes and focused eyes, fogged eyes and glazed eyes—wipes his own eyes on his shirt hem, which is caked with bits of old ejaculations, days of built-up crusts of rubbings of his parts.

He's never seen Kate McClane's eyes. He's only seen the Perfect Breasts. He makes an avatar of educated guesses. Size and shape.

The color of her skin—he's seen her skin, of course, but it's distorted in the image by the shadows and the flash. The cut and texture of her hair—the picture shows a little sliver of a slipped strand, like she's pulled it up and just beyond his view. Her mouth, her lips—he's never seen, but he conjures an image from the soft curve of her neck, the hollows of her throat.

He scrolls, and scrolls, and clicks, and scrolls, and

clicks—each *click-click-click-click* is her whisper—
What do you want? What is wrong with you?—He
answers with an all-wrong woman's shape. He dresses
it in different costumes. Shells of armor. Sheaths of
velvet. Skins of dirty rags.

He clicks them on and off. And on. And off.
He clicks her non-form naked.
Clicks her naked non-form left and right.
Distant.
Then close.
Hovers above her.
Zooms in—closer, closer, *click-click-click-click*—til
he's close as he can get, looking into the non-eyes of
the non-face he has made.

—

Outside, a zombie lies like dripped wax. Limbs spilt down the alley. Filth-annealed. Stiff-soft. Jaw drooped so far down his face looks melted open. Gray-tooth-gapped around the black bowl of his mouth. The holes of his shirt, frayed, congealing in the hot goop of his sores. Even now, in his sleep, he feels pain, feels his wrong parts. Raw from overuse and underuse. He tastes metallic spit-snot running down his throat. He smells his skin, still burning underneath the black sky, razing red beneath the black sky, oozing out into the dark.

—

That night, she lies deep in the red drifts of her waiting-sickness, fingering the nubs of pilled up mesh built up along the shirt's hem, skin stretched hard against this swollen ache—this hard heat in her head—that feels like it's pressing into every pore. The room is hot. The oscillating fan just breathes more heat. It whispers heat. It whispers in the soft warm hiss-spit of Marianne Lee. It goes, *shhhhhhh, click, shhhhhhh click, shhhhhhh click, I have…shhhhhhh, click, shhhhhhh click, shhhhhhh, click,—I have a huge…*

She runs her hand beneath the shirt. She feels her flushed bumps, irritated nipples, tufts of just-beginning-to-grow hair. The itches, pricks of just-becoming, the discomforts of this just-becoming—just becoming, what? Just, *just*. A small thing. Something barely. No. She wants the slick-tongued grinning of Marianne Lee, whatever's under all that confidence. The knowing look that melts, sometimes, like it's just too delicious to contain. It's really sad—she realizes—that she's known Marianne Lee for years, but still knows so, so little of the things she knows—now—that she wants to know—she *needs* to know, like how she manages to get her hair into those perfect waves, like what she likes to eat, like what she's most afraid of, what she wants to be when she grows up, how she has grown, and where she's grown, is she afraid of all this growth and all this change, is she afraid to grow up, does she have some image in her mind, does she know what she means when she says, *huge cock?*

The hard heat builds to such a painful swell, she sits up in her bed. But she feels clear now, shedding sweat. She knows now what she needs. So, she gets up. Creeps softly. Runs her hand along the shadows of the walls, and feels her way down to her father's den.

—

How soft, the movement that emerges from this stillness.

How soft, the echoes of the clock.

How soft, the night-dark rustle of the drapes.

How soft, the stirring of these objects as you touch them, one by one, wondering if they've moved, or if you've moved—and are you moving?

So, so softly radiating. *With the energy within things.*

So, so softly gleaming. *With the shifting shape inside the mirror.*

So, so softly pulsing. *With the fear of what's within things.*

With the fear of bumping into your own shadow in the dark.

—

He stands—sweat-soaked and naked—in the dark, amidst the blue drones of the fridge, the door wide open, holding it out, looking, looking, looking in, and soaking in the fake frost, fake cold, getting his skin pricked with fake chill, shivering fake shivers, feeling hungry, feeling numb. Somehow, he always has a lot of food, but never any real food, nothing substantial, nothing that could go with anything else, make a meal, like, the kind of thing you eat while sitting down. He eats between pinched fingers—goblin-blue—while standing up. Pinches of shredded cheese, green olives—sucking cold brine from his fingertips—a gulp of milk—a phlegmy flavor starts to lubricate his throat—a slice of stiff bread, dipped into some mild, recently expired salsa. For dessert, a stick of foil-wrapped margarine.

He needs a job, he thinks, but getting jobs has always felt like filling up his fridge, some strange, amorphous process, rules he has never understood, and—yes—somehow, he always ends up with a bunch

of shit he doesn't want—but has to put—inside of him.
He cracks the window just enough to smoke the last of
his Virginia Slims. He sucks in, breathes out, sucks in,
breathes out, ashes through the crack. The air outside
of him is smoke. The air inside of him is smoke. It
looks and smells and tastes and feels the fucking same.

—

She goes back to the same chatroom for gay men, 21-30. A/S/Ls herself as: 22/M/California.

Where in California? Types a 24/M/Dayton, OH.

The beach, she types.

He types back, you sound hot.

I am, she types. She searches, *California surfer hot guy*. Sends the seventh image that comes up: a dope in surf trunks. Pouty mouth. Trim. Tan. A little greasy. Bad teeth. Dumbass-looking bowl cut. Hot, but not too hot. She thinks, yeah, I think I could be that guy.

You need a hair cut, types back 24/M/Dayton.

I know, she types. My mom is always telling me to get it cut.

Your body's good, though, he types. Firm and skinny, like I like.

She feels proud. She thinks, I know. I chose that picture well.

She asks, what do you look like? Thinking, haha, he is from Ohio. So, he's maybe small town-hot, but not as hot as me. She sits and waits for him to send an image, goose-bumped legs crossed in the swivel chair, her mesh shirt hem hitched, brushing at her ribcage. The collar of the shirt half crumpled in her mouth. She nibbles at it, nervously, and chew-sucks its synthetic threads.

She gets a file labeled, me.jpg.

She clicks it open.

It's a picture of his penis in his hand.

It is a pale, hairy hand. It is a long, thin, pasty penis. Pink and bald. It looks upset to be there, in the photo, in his hand.

She hiss-sucks harder on her shirt mesh, feels a little sick. Like how she feels when she has been sick for a long time. Like when she's been in bed, deep-covered in the dark, and feels nauseous, but the hollow-hunger starts to overtake everything else.

You like?

The cursor goes, *blink, blink, blink*, as she thinks about it. Does she like? And what, exactly, does she? He? The he she wants to be? She knows *she* likes nothing she sees, there, in that photo. Doesn't like the hairy hand, the flash, the way the pink glares raw. But she likes thinking of *his* hand—smooth fingers, sand grit underneath his nails—and his/her/his hunger catching like a hang nail in his gut, and yes, she/he/she likes the thought of his/her/his bright-swelling warmth, and yes, she/he/she likes the thought of his/her/his *huge cock*.

—

Outside, the zombie stirs. The first thing that he feels is the scraping of the wall, the gray grit mortar of the brick behind his back. His ashy flecks of skin. He moves his mouth and tastes bacteria. He swallows streams of heated organisms. Not-him. Now-becoming-him. His fingers claw half-consciously inside his pockets as he squints up at the black sky, not sure if it's early morning, late night, neither, if the blackness that he sees is sky, or smoke-black, both, and his not-knowing fills him with a sudden fear.

He braces himself, presses hands into hot gravel, brick grit, scuffles to his feet, strips of his shredded pant legs dragging on the ground. He looks around him—brick wall, dumpster, other zombies, street sign, gas station, the highway exit, mountains in the distance, highway exit, gas station, street sign, and other zombies, dumpster, brick wall—and he thinks, I need to move. I need to get to things.

He needs: something to eat.

He needs: something to drink.

He needs: something to keep the sky from burning.

He needs: shelter so he doesn't burn.

He needs: to move until he finds a place that isn't dark, somewhere where he can see the sky, and read the signals of the sky.

―

How soft, the movement that emerges from this stillness.

How soft, the blending of the blackness all around you.

How soft, the dream-numb steps you take, not knowing why, or where you're going.

How soft, the slow, slow, spreading of the open road behind you.

So, so softly radiating. *With the energy within things.*

So, so softly gleaming. *With heat vapors, drawing life into the air.*

So, so softly pulsing. *With the fear of what's within things.*

With the fear of now becoming
even more
inhuman.

—

In his computer, he has kept a folder labeled *Kate*. The folder *Kate* consists of dozens of zip files with porn. Kate McClane used to send this porn to him without an explanation beyond cryptic messages like: *This is what I'm into.*

He clicks an image of a woman in a suitcase. Parts chopped up and organized in tidy little rows.

He clicks an image of a woman in a bath tub full of viscera.

He clicks an image of a woman lying in an alley.

He clicks an image of a headless woman on a meat hook. She is nude, but for a garter belt, black stockings, pointed patent heels. Her gleaming body dangled, twisted, murdered in mid-motion, one leg bent seductively, the other dripping wet with piss. The meat hook pierces through the space between her shining, swollen breasts. Her hands are dwarfed by them, and clasped above them, shoulders drawn protectively. Her severed head is underneath the drizzled piss leg. Her long blonde hair is splayed out in the splatter. She has a very strange expression one could read as almost anything. It could be shame (For what? For getting caught? Discovered in some indiscretion?). Or, acceptance of her death, a look of sadness as she realizes she's about to die. Or, it could also be—and this is what he most often decides upon, when zooming closer, closer, to the severed head, there, on his screen—a look of disappointment, quiet judgement, like she's thinking, *Why? Why are you doing that? What are you doing? What is wrong with you?*

He never touches himself, looking at these pictures. He just scans around them, clicking closer, closer, to see all the details. The spaces in-between his joints—his cartilage—now tingling, the access points, the dotted lines that would be severed. He forces himself to imagine how each cut would feel. How much he'd feel, at first—a pain so overwhelming that he almost wouldn't feel it through the shock—and then, a pain that would be mostly aftershock, the registration of pain upon pain, already almost-felt. But never fully felt, though, when you think about it. Isn't that the thing about pain, how your body never lets you fully recognize what it is feeling, never lets you really feel it, how your body—even your own body—never lets you in.

—

She creeps back to her father's chair, back to the black box, to the ghost-hiss-shrieking shivers of anticipation of connection. She finds a 26/M/Creve Coeur, MO. This time, gets right to the point. She types, hey there. I want to see your cock.

She gets an image labeled 219634.jpg. Clicks. It's a large file, and the image loads so slowly. She gets a bit of forehead—what looks like a bandage—is he bleeding?—no, a wet white towel—curly damp hair—closed eyes—kinda weak chin—silver chain necklace—now, little pinprick nipples—ripples, ripples, gradually shaping into muscles, into shapes that meld together—an intense V-muscle there, and there, and there, still going—just below his belly button—suddenly—WHOA! Big huge cock!

26/M/Creve Coeur types, now, let's see yours.

She types, wait a minute while I get my camera.

She does a search for *hot thin guy medium cock*. It takes awhile to find an image of a guy she doesn't hate. She settles on a picture that is cut-off at the eyes. A thin and lightly toned guy, modest tan, a trail of dark, feathery hair. A half-hard cock propped up against his unzipped jeans, made to look bigger than it is. And, in the background, you can see a stack of Charmin toilet paper, and a bottle of Pantene Pro-V conditioner. Hot, but not too hot. She thinks, yeah, I could be that guy.

Goddamn, types 26/M/Creve Coeur. I am rock hard, now.

Me too, she types. She thinks about what that would mean. She feels rock hard in her stomach and leg muscles: tensed, but weirdly calm. She thinks, Marianne Lee would be so proud of me.

I'm running my tongue down your chest. I'm sucking on your nipples. Do you like that? 26/M/Creve Coeur types.

To her surprise, she gasps. She types back, yes. I'm gasping.

He types back, that's good. I want you hot and hard and begging for it.

She doesn't know what *it* will be, so she types, okay, I am ready.

Are you begging for it?

Yes, I'm begging for it.

Show me how you beg, he types.

She knows what begging looks like, so she types: Hands clasped together. Eyes closed tight. I whisper, please, please, please, please, please.

He clicks through Craigslist job posts labeled *etc/misc*. He's naked and unshaven. Prickled dusks of little hairs. Red bumps of irritation. Sleep studies. Cancer studies. Psychiatric studies. Selling plasma. Something labeled *Qualified Spray Techniton*. A bunch of *Personal Assistant* gigs that sound like ads for sex, for *female, fit, attractive, age 18-21, photo required*. He finds an ad for *Medical Driver*, and out of curiosity, he clicks to see what that might mean. He doesn't get much: *Help needed for med-related transport. Miles reimbursed.* Serious inquiries, it says, should go to Dwayne.

He calls the number. Gets an answer on the first ring. This is Dwayne.

Hi, Dwayne. I'm curious about—

Dwayne interrupts, it's for a driver, but you'll mostly ride along when we do pick-ups. What we need is someone with a license and some…Here, Dwayne pauses…flexibility.

I'm flexible, he says.

That's good, says Dwayne.

I have a license, he says.

Good, says Dwayne. Let's get you in, then, for an interview.

Dwayne gives a day, a time, an address, and checks three times to make sure he writes it down, which he does, on the nearest surface. The nearest surface is the backside of the photo of the Perfect Breasts. He tapes the photo backwards to the mirror, so he won't forget.

After a series of these late night visits to her father's den, she learns new skills, acquires a strange new secret language. She keeps a notebook where she writes each word she doesn't know, and writes each definition as it is revealed to her.

Blowjob = sucking cock

Go down on = sucking cock

Giving head = sucking cock

Face fucking = sucking cock

While she's researching terms, she finds a step-by-step list that describes—in great detail—*the proper blowjob etiquette procedure:*

1. Start out with a little teasing. Give his cock a few strokes.

2. Slowly unbutton and unzip his pants with your teeth.

3. Swirl your tongue around his cock head for 10-20 seconds.

4. Spread your saliva, alternating between up and down, and round strokes.

5. Gently massage his balls with your free hand (DO NOT FORGET THIS STEP!)

6. Glide your teeth lightly (lightly!) one time along his shaft.

7. Make eye contact for 7 seconds. Smile devilishly (no sad puppy eyes!).

8. Make sure you are hitting just the right spot underneath the head.

9. Work your way deep, deep, deep as you can go without puking.

10. If he says that he's about to come, pick up your pace.

11. When he comes, slowly move your mouth backward. Swallow. Lick off any excess.

12. Congratulations! You just gave a blowjob!

She writes the word *shaft* in her dictionary. Reads each step a second time. Closes her eyes and tries to picture unbuttoning pants with teeth, and how to move your eyes, your lips, and tilt your head to smile *devilishly* while your mouth is very busy. This is a lot of work, she thinks, learning this language, memorizing all these steps, let alone actually doing them. It will be worth it, though, she thinks, if she can she can use what she is learning, and she will—she will use all of it—on Marianne Lee.

The zombie walks along the highway, moving out in the direction of the mountains' sloped forms in the fog, toward their golden glow, toward what some part of him knows must be the source of all this heat, the smell of ore, the smell of blisters, smell of death. He sees the silhouettes of low-growth, blackened streaks among the brush, like slashes, scratches, scars, the slit skins of the earth. He sees the way these streaks trace to the shadows of the pines, the smoke that grows more thick, more potent, pine-sharp, rich with all the growth that it consumes. He sees a blood-bright, red-orange circle, buried deep inside the smoke, and he can't tell if it's the sunrise, or the center of the flames. He holds his arms out, and he cups his hands around the distant shape, as though to clasp it and to carry it inside of him.

She holds the door open for Marianne Lee when she knocks. Marianne Lee is wearing dark tights, combat boots, and fishnet hand gloves even in the heat. Her mouth twists in amusement and confusion. What, why are you hiding, little creeper? You don't need to hide. They climb the carpeted half flight of stairs to her embarrassing room with its rose wallpaper and its grandma-lacy curtains. They sit across from one another on her creaky daybed, fidgeting, not really hearing what they say to one another. Marianne Lee puts her hand on a loose bed knob and pops it off. She says, you could keep things inside here, if you wanted. She puts it back, and says a little bit more quietly, well, at least, if I lived here, that's what I would do.

Her mother brings an unromantic meal of cheese puffs, Diet Rite, and mini-corndogs on a tray with a near-empty plastic bottle of some off-brand ketchup that they have to strangle-squeeze to get anything out of, and it goes *split-splittle-splurt*. Marianne Lee fake-coughs like she is choking as she splurts her ketchup. Dips a mini-corndog, nibbles with surprising daintiness.

I know, don't tell me. I eat like a weird old lady.

No, it's cute, she says.

Neither of them knows how they should respond to her response.

You said you had something to show me? Marianne Lee almost whispers.

She bends down, so she is almost brushing Marianne Lee's boots. She pulls a composition notebook from beneath the bed. She opens it, and passes it to Marianne Lee with a pen.

The first page of the notebook says:

21/M/European. Hello, I am new here, an exchange student. I'm hoping to explore the world with you. I'm 6' 4", dark, handsome, athletic. Romantic, for the most part, but sometimes I can get a little wild. By the way, I am a switch. I can be dominant and fierce, or I can let you take control of me, if you desire. Come let me whisper in your ear. Let me enchant you. Let me slowly undress you, discover all the secrets of your body. I promise I will be as gentle as you like. I promise I will make it worth your while.

Marianne Lee makes a sound like, *ha!* Puts a hand

over her mouth. She waves her other hand like, *just forget I did that.* She watches Marianne Lee's eyes get wide, then wider, scanning back and forth, over and over, down along the page. Marianne Lee's tongue runs across her teeth. She rubs her lips together, like she's chewing on an invisible string of licorice. She thumbs the pen cap so it goes *cli-click, cli-click.* She puts the pen cap in her mouth. She bites down. Swallows. Starts to write.

He goes to the address Dwayne gave, which takes him to an outdoor coffee stand with two small plastic tables with small plastic chairs. He sits in one, and waits. Two kids who look too young to be there by themselves are sitting at the other, coloring a stack of books. Not coloring books, but a stack of regular print novels, which, he notices, all have library barcodes on the sides. Meanwhile, of course, the atmosphere is wrong. The day-sky is still black—still smells of burning—and the air is thick with smog.

A man who must be Dwayne pulls up and parks his motorcycle. Dwayne has shoulder-length gray hair half-bundled in a messy bun. Dwayne shakes his hand, but doesn't make eye contact as he does. He sits across from him and doesn't order anything.

So, as I said, Dwayne says, this job is for someone to help with pick-ups, which take place in hospitals, old folks' homes, houses, trailers. Sometimes, open fields. Any time of day or night. You never know, of course. And that is why we need someone who's flexible.

By pick-ups, what do you mean? I mean, what exactly are we picking up? He asks, although somehow he knows already. That is why he came.

Dwayne says, dead bodies. Yeah. *Dead bodies,* he repeats, using a whisper-hiss that's louder than the voice that he was using.

The kids don't seem to hear, and if they do, they don't care. They sit silent at their table, scrawling with their broken crayons.

What do we pick them up in? He asks. I mean, in what kind of vehicle?

A van, says Dwayne. A black van. It's my van.

And is there training? What is that like? He asks.

First time, it's a ride-along, says Dwayne. You know. To see if this is something you would want to do.

Dwayne pauses. Is this something you would want to do?

He says, maybe. I think. I don't know. I think that I need to know more.

Dwayne slowly nods, like he has had this conversation many times. Most people probably don't make it past this part.

He feels a twinge of pride that he has made it past this part. He feels shivers of some dread-excitement prickling the insides of his chest, his neck. Like loose internal threads. The scraping scribbles of the broken crayons becomes the shifting of these threads, the rhythms of his thoughts.

What do you need to know? Dwayne asks, using a tone of studied calm.

I don't know…everything? Like, how do I know when there is a pick-up?

I will call you, Dwayne says, calmly. I will give you one hour's notice. I will say, pick-up downtown, in the city, in the county. I will tell you if it is a natural death, suicide, or accident. He pauses. Or…if it is something else.

What do you mean by…something else? He asks. He feels a shiver creeping in his throat and wishes that he'd ordered something from the stand.

I mean—Dwayne leans in, looks over his shoulder at the kids, and whisper-hisses—sometimes, they are not *whole* bodies, if you know what I mean. Sometimes, someone will report a hand, a leg, some kind of...part—or parts—that they found decomposing in a field. And, so, we have to kinda... gather them. Dwayne pinches his hand through the air in front of them, gathering invisible parts.

What do we use to...pick up parts? He asks.

Bags, Dwayne says. Big black bags, you know. With zippers. And I use gloves. Vinyl gloves, because I have a latex allergy. Some people like to wear a mask, but I don't wear one. You get used to smells. You just build up a tolerance.

What do you wear for pick-ups? He asks, picturing hazmat suits, plastic ponchos, meat aprons and face shields, some kind of protection.

Dwayne looks down and thinks about it. Maybe like...a polo shirt? Some khakis?

He cannot imagine Dwayne wearing a pair of khakis.

Dwayne's voice gets lower. Now, I need to level with you. In this job, you will get blood on you. And bits of skin. And bits of peoples' insides. Bits of brain. You will see splattered bits. You will see death of all kinds, and decay of all kinds. Maggots. You will see *dead babies*.

The two crayon-scribbling kids perk up at the sound of *dead babies*. They look at one another, snort-laugh, scurry off to who the fuck knows where. They are alone, now. Him and Dwayne. Here at their plastic table, underneath the black sky, surrounded on all sides by soon-to-be deaths. Dwayne still has not made any eye contact. He looks down at the ground on his left side, like he is watching something crawling in the dirt. Slick strands of gray hair hang over his eyes, concealing them. Thick beads of sweat drip, likely darkening the same spot.

I need to tell you about my first ride-along, Dwayne says. The call came, and they said it was a suicide. They said a guy had killed himself at home, in his garage, inside his car. So, I was picturing a simple clean-up, figuring he'd closed the door, and gassed himself. I got there, and I saw these cop cars in his driveway, red lights flashing, saw the people moving in and out of his house, in the dark. I thought, why do they need so many people for a guy who killed himself like that, alone in his garage? And then, I saw why. For some reason, he had sat down in his driver's seat, and

blown his brains out—you know, with a gun—there,
in his car. His face was not a face. There was this shell
of what had been a face. Like, from the left side, if you
looked in through the window, in the dark, it was a
face, still. On the left side, he still had one eye, one ear,
some hair, and even enough jaw, there, that the face
still had a face shape. But on the right side—and if you
looked in, then, through the windshield, you would
see—this blast of bloody flesh and tissue, just this
cave of splattered mess. And it did something to me,
seeing someone's face like that. This splattered mess
just sitting there on top of normal shoulders, arms, and
chest. It was the strangest thing, helping to haul him
out, shifting his arms and shoulders, feeling all these
whole and normal muscles in my hands, then looking
up, every so often, and just seeing…that. And I looked
up because the bits—the flecks of muscle, fat, and
brain—would drip down on my face as I was moving
him around. I even got a bit of bloody brain inside my
mouth, at one point. You'll learn to keep your mouth
closed at this job, I'll tell you that. Dwayne makes a
weird laugh that does not sound like a laugh.

Dwayne doesn't talk for what feels like a long and heavy moment, which he needs. He shuts his eyes. Imagines flapped skin, shards of bone, red sludge, pink-yellow flecks of fat, stiff shoulders, dead-weight arms beneath—he would be wearing a red flannel shirt, he thinks, yes, he feels sure of this—small drips of red blood blending in amidst the flannel, sticky froths among the carpet, crusted on the ceiling. Drips of brain—oh god—a dark metallic flavor fills his mouth. He runs his tongue around the insides of his cheeks, the sour slicks of his teeth, tastes it—yes, the warm-cold, weird wet, shocks of recognition, someone else's insides, on the outside, suddenly—now, suddenly—inside of him. He can imagine all of this, and feel all of this, with such ease that he thinks, god, I could *do* this. I'd be good at this.

So, how much does it pay? He asks.

It's $30 for a pick-up, Dwayne says.

$30 an hour?

No, for the whole pick-up.

And...how many of those do you do...like, in a normal week?

Dwayne shrugs. You never know. Sometimes, none. Sometimes, there'll be dozens. In times like this, the heat, the fire, you'll get a lot of calls. Old folks and junkies dying. He points at the black sky. 'Tis the season.

He finds himself saying, I'd like to do a ride-along.

Dwayne nods. I had a feeling about you. So, now, the only thing I need here is a background check. Dwayne passes him a grainy one-page form that looks like its been recopied for several decades. It takes less than 30 seconds to fill out the whole thing. Dwayne takes it and nods again. Well, you'll be hearing from me.

As Dwayne remounts his motorcycle, brushes back his hair, he finally makes eye contact. His eyes are milky blue.

One more thing, Dwayne says. I don't say this to be morbid, but I really love my job. I really do love what I do

---

The red-orange circle seems closer and closer, brighter and brighter. The zombie stares ahead, eyes locked around it, hardly noticing the blurs of passing cars, the blares of car horns wailing, even semi trucks that swerve away from him at the last moment. The air is so hot that he feels like his lungs are bursting open from the inside, filling fuller with each breath he takes. The blonde hairs of the hills bend like an unseen hand is sifting slender fingers through them—searchingly—then brushing them aside.

———

She finds the chatroom and she finds Marianne Lee there. It is easy. They are labeled as they both said they would be:

21/M/Kansas City, KS (That's her.)

21/M/Saskatoon, SK (That's Marianne Lee.)

Hey there, types Marianne Lee.

Hey there, she types.

You sound hot, types Marianne Lee.

You too, she types. Giggles. She types, let's go fuck.

Marianne Lee types, soooo...what are you wearing?

She pauses and thinks about it. Searches, *hot guy casual outfit*. Most of the images that come up are of tight blue jeans and white t-shirts. She types, a worn-in white tee. Smells like sweat. A pair of tight blue jeans. They're bulging right now, in a certain spot that's really straining. And a belt, but...(Unbuckles the belt and slides it off).

Marianne Lee types, (Takes belt from your hands, loops belt behind your neck to pull you closer).

She types, wow, feeling a little forward, are we?

Marianne Lee types (Kisses you deeply).

She types, (Kisses back, sliding a little tongue in).

Marianne Lee types back, (Smiles into kiss).

—

The zombie has now reached a quiet stretch of road.

If he were to look back, he'd see a panorama of the city from above.

The tall sepulchers of the factories.

The sunset-colored neon, gray-haze, drone-hum flickers of the lights.

He'd likely see the shadowed shoulders of that high rise building where, so long ago—so deep within those dark throbs of his memories—he had some kind of childhood, he had some kind of family, he had some kind of home, some long ago-lived life.

But he does not look back.

He looks toward the red-orange circle.

Moves toward the red-orange circle.

Thinking non-thoughts of the red-orange circle.

Thinking non-thoughts only of the red-orange circle.

Feeling non-feelings of red-orange glow and red-orange warmth and red-orange life.

—

He's kept another folder labeled *Conversations*. It is filled with messages from him to Kate, from Kate to him, a script-like back and forth, an invisible play, a strange performance taking place inside two separate minds from many miles away.

They wrote about so many things, and—at the same time—they were always the same things, essentially: *I don't feel right, living where I live. I don't feel right, living inside this body. I don't feel right with anyone, anywhere, and I want to die.*

And it was always ultimately about Kate McClane, not him. He was a listener, at best. Mostly, an audience.

She'd write, I feel like shit today.

And he'd write, yeah?

And she'd write, yeah. I heated up a paring knife and pressed the hot tip to my clit.

She is—or was—so full of herself. Writing like some femme fatale, like every fucking thing she did was just so interesting. Yes, he knew—he knows—that she was writing to all kinds of guys. That's why he asked for her to send the photo of the Perfect Breasts.

She is—or was—a real person. He knows that. He's tried so hard to picture her as real, imagine real things that she might do. As he moves through his day, he asks himself questions about Kate McClane, answers himself in his inner version of her voice. Like how much milk she pours into her cereal. He figures she would only use a little bit. She'd like the flakes to stay hard, sharp. He wonders if she prefers taking baths, or showers. He thinks she most likely bathes, spends long, dark moments underwater. Fills the bath with water that is scalding hot, then waits until it's ice cold, sitting, arms around her knees, as it goes groaning down the drain.

All day, he carries it: the weight of what he doesn't know.

All day, he shifts his mind, his muscles, to absorb this weight.

All day, he looks at himself, picturing himself as her.

All day, he punishes himself in small ways for being Not-Kate-McClane.

Like, for example—now—when scrolling through the *Conversations* files. He finds a conversation from five months ago, when she was writing—as she often did—about her thoughts of dying, thoughts that never felt quite real to him, although he knew they must be real to her.

I used to think that I should go out with some big performance.

Yeah?

You know, some gory spectacle. Like, metal hooks under my ribs and guts, then jump off of a building so it all goes flying out in some big gross explosion. Something confrontational like that.

You changed your mind, though?

I don't know. It's hard to tell if I just want something because somebody else would think that it's the kind of thing I'd do. But lately, I've been feeling kind of quiet, like I want to just curl up in some dark corner, like a cat, and die alone.

Reading these messages, he now remembers how he thought, then, If you want to just curl up in some dark corner, die alone, then why are you contacting

66

me, why are you telling me, or asking me, why don't you fucking do it, if that's what you want to do? But now, he realizes she was as confused as he was. More so. She had so many more voices in her head, saying *yeah, what, oh, you sound sexy, and I like that, and what are you wearing, doing, feeling, thinking, are you thinking of me, right now, touching yourself thinking of me, right now, have you been a good girl, have you been a bad girl, have you been thinking of me, what are you thinking?* He wants to know. He wants to think it for himself-herself. He wants to see her when he looks at himself in the mirror. Catches his reflection in the screen, the dark, the blue-dim glow. Catches the hard hook of the otherness—the *him*-ness—of his thoughts.

And so, he stands naked before the mirror with a black marker.

He draws a set of dashed dark lines across his thighs.

He draws another dashed line midway through his stomach, where his guts are.

Draws two more, across his arms, the tender undersides of his joints.

He draws two lines under his knee caps and two lines around his wrists.

And, finally, a dashed line through the Adam's Apple of his throat.

He stares at his divided, dashed-up self.

He sees the softness of his belly.

Sees the bulges of his veins.

Traces the bulges with the tips of his nails.

Shudders.

Steps back.

Looks away.

He thinks, I'm a coward. I'm a coward. I'm a coward.

—

The sky has dimmed from black.

To darker black.

To blackest black.

The red-orange circle looming ever-bright.

Cars rush by.

Unseen.

Unheard.

Occasionally, people in the cars look out and point.

Hey, isn't that a person?

Isn't there a person, back there?

—

21/M/Saskatoon, SK has now gone silent.

21/M/Kansas City, KS has now gone silent.

She waits.

Legs curled into her chest.

Chin pressed into her knees.

She stares hard at the cold glow of the now unchanging screen.

―

He paces back and forth.

He looks toward the phone.

Opens the fridge and peels the wrapping from a block of stale cheese.

He looks toward the phone.

Listens and hears the humming of the fridge.

Listens and hears the humming of his overheated monitor.

Listens and hears the *tap, tap,* tapping of the leaky tap.

He looks toward the phone.

He stands before the mirror.

Reminds himself of all his parts.

His dashed lines.

Looks toward the phone.

Looks toward the dashed lines.

Looks toward the phone.

Looks toward the dashed lines.

Looks toward the phone.

—

Marianne Lee types—finally—you are so good at this. You're really, really good at this.

And—for the first time—she wonders what *this* might mean.

What it might mean, to be so good at being someone you created.

And so bad at being anything—anyone—else.

—

The zombie hears the sound of rushed air, metal, force colliding with his flesh before the burst, before the blooms of skin, before the gush of veins, before the crack of bones, before the streams of blood, before the pierce, the slit, the split, the splinter, splatter, spray, before the spreading out and separation of internal from external, before he is bits of debris, before he is scattered parts.

The phone rings.

It is Dwayne.

Dwayne says, pick-up, out in the county. It's a big one. I mean, bad one. Are you ready?

He looks at his reflection, fingering the dashed line of his throat.

He watches himself swallow.

He says, yes.

Marianne Lee comes wearing black pants and a white button-down shirt, just like they talked about. She also wears a black and white striped tie. The tie is loosely knotted, dangling askew across her chest, like she is trying to conceal her ineptitude for tying ties.

Like Marianne Lee, she is wearing black pants and a white blouse, but her only white blouse is a work shirt that her father used to wear. It is enormous, so she's wearing it untucked with leggings and an earring in one ear, like it's a look she's going for.

You're both dressed up, her mother remarks warily, bringing a tray with iced Sweet'n Low tea, and plates of pizza bagel bites.

We're practicing for our adulthood. Marianne Lee pops a pizza bagel in her mouth and locks the bedroom door.

—

He looks toward the dashed lines in the mirror.

Then, he eats the bottom quarter of an old, expired jar of salsa.

The salsa tastes like putrid chunks of vinegar: cold, burning, damp, and bitter.

It's the perfect thing for him to eat.

He reads his final massage from Kate McClane, from four months ago, the one that had an eerie tone of pre-preparedness.

Thank you for listening to me. For being out there, when I feel trapped inside myself, whatever this self is. I've been here long enough. I've done this long enough. I think I'm ready to see what else there might be, if anything.

He looks, again, toward the dashed lines in the mirror. Taps his nail against the flip side of the photo of the Perfect Breasts. Closes his eyes, and pictures them, now, after four months of decay: deflating bulbs of bright, wine-colored muscle, roots of blue vein, sloughs of parchment-dry skin, yellow-gray, and blackened, filled with little burrows—maybe one, there, in the crevice of the base—and one, there underneath the puffed shell of the shape that was the nipple—with their ever-shifting sticky lace of drips of teams of moving maggots.

He thinks about dead bodies.

Thinks about dead bodies in a field.

Thinks about dead parts.

Thinks about parts.

Thinks about parting and partitioning.

Thinks about picking the parts up.

Thinks about picking the parts up, looking at them, holding them in his hands.

———

They're lying in the dark.

She and Marianne Lee.

She's lying on her daybed, on her back, face turned toward the ceiling.

Marianne Lee is lying on the floor, below her, in her sleeping bag. She's also on her back, face turned toward the ceiling.

The ceiling's covered with glow-in-the-dark stickers of stars and planets, all her favorite constellations. Ursa Major with its pointy head, its leaping legs. The Hydra with its sprawling, snaking zig-zag of a body. Gemini, the two twins holding hands.

She starts.

She whispers—barely whispers—her lips shivering, my cock is hard.

How hard? Asks Marianne Lee.

So, so hard.

They lie there for another long and silent moment, looking at the shapes of constellations in the fake night sky.

I'm stroking it, Marianne Lee whispers. Your cock. I'm stroking it with just my finger tips. Back and forth. Up and down.

I'm moaning as you do that, she lowers her voice, and tries to moan, but it comes out sounding more like a stifled sneeze.

Now, I'm unbuckling your belt. Unbuttoning your pants. Unzipping them. I'm taking your cock in my hands. The full length of your cock.

You…you should take my cock, she sucks in air. She coughs. The tip of my cock. Put it in your mouth. And run your tongue…around it.

I'm running my tongue all around the tip of your cock. It is warm, Marianne Lee says.

How warm? She asks.

So, so warm. And wet.

And, now, she breathes, take it in deeper. Deeper in your throat.

She hears Marianne Lee clearing her throat. She gulps. Imagines how her spit tastes.

She looks down. Marianne Lee's eyes are closed. Her lips are pressed together, tightly. Both her hands

79

are tucked inside the sleeping bag. The sleeping bag is making little rustle-crinkles as Marianne Lee moves in it. Undulating. Slow, rolling rotations.

That feels…she squints, rummaging through her memory, trying to find some tantalizing words. She gives up. So, so good.

Marianne Lee nods, like she's actually doing what they're saying she is doing, and imagining she's doing.

I want to fuck you, she whispers, emboldened by the word. She feels it like a hissing fizz that's frothing through her inner liquids. I want to fuck you. Will you let me? Will you let me? Fuck you?

Yes, Marianne Lee says in a high-pitched, breathy voice she's never heard her use.

Marianne Lee's lips are parted open. Slick and shining. Gleaming teeth. Tongue tipped behind them, like a little trigger.

She pushes back the covers of the daybed, pushes them aside, extracts her legs, sits up, and edges toward Marianne Lee. The hissing fizz fills all her movements with a frozen-muscle-dead-limbs-waking-up-and-not-yet-working sort of tingling.

She kneels down beside the sleeping bag.

She leans in.

Marianne Lee opens her eyes.

Closes them.

And leans in too.

She presses her mouth to her mouth.

It's warm.

And wet.

She runs her tongue over her mouth.

Inside her mouth.

Along her tongue.

She feels the quickening of Marianne Lee's breath.

She feels her moving in the sleeping bag.

She feels her pulse.

A twitch.

Marianne Lee's tongue twitches.

But she doesn't move her mouth.

Marianne Lee puts her hands on her shoulders — gently—like she is trying to pull her in closer, closer, closer…

But, she doesn't.

Marianne Lee hovers, hesitating, crinkling around,

pulse pounding, wordless, breathing, before pushing her away.

I'm sorry, Marianne Lee says. I don't know why. I wanted to. I thought I wanted to. But, I just don't feel anything.

―

He thinks about dead bodies.

Thinks about thin light beams in the dark.

Thinks about tall grass, insects, whispering.

Thinks about dry grass, bristling.

Thinks about charred smell, smoke, and ash.

Thinks about small, soft, careful steps.

Thinks about big black bags that will be filled.

Thinks about squinting, searching.

Thinks about looking, noticing.

Thinks about the mix of stillness, subtle movement.

Thinks about suddenly seeing it.

Thinks about them.

Thinks about parts.

Thinks about limbs.

Thinks about skull.

Thinks about bone.

Thinks about brain.

Thinks about skin, separate from bone.

Thinks about bone, separate from muscle, skin.

Thinks about smelling it.

Thinks about how the smell would seep.

Thinks about how the smell would fill his head.

Thinks about how the smell would taste inside his mouth.

Thinks about licking at his teeth, as though to clean himself.

Thinks about gray, umbilical-like intestines.

Thinks about red-spew matter.

Thinks about the bright of it, shining inside his flashlight.

Thinks about picking it up.

Thinks about fingers, scraping.

Thinks about the feel of that.

Thinks about warmth and cold and wetness in his hands.

Thinks about getting used to it.

Thinks about bending, scraping, scooping without thinking.

Thinks about beginning to see all of this as nothing.

Thinks about maybe beginning to enjoy it.

Thinks about maybe beginning to identify with it.

Thinks about never thinking, caring, wanting to be

touched by someone else.

Thinks about never thinking, caring, wanting to touch anything alive.

Thinks about wanting to be dead.

Thinks about wanting to be dead.

Thinks about wanting to be dead.

Thinks about wanting, only, ever, to be dead.

He grabs his clothing, throws it over himself, rushing out the door.

He pounds down stairs, through halls, half-runs into the street.

He pushes through the alley, past the zombies with slumped shoulders, shredded clothes.

He wanders through the beams of street lamps, batting moths, and snows of ash.

He wanders til he sees the flickering of neon diner signs that read: open 24 hours-a-day.

He sits down in a booth. Orders a stack of six buttermilk pancakes.

He arranges all the half-n-half containers in a pyramid.

He gets the pancakes.

Holds the syrup glass above them.

Watches syrup drizzle down them, over them, into, around them, in a daze.

He shoves them in his mouth, sawing the side of his fork, barely even chewing.

Poking his gums with the tines.

The metal mixed with butter, sugar, sweet fluff.

Swallowing.

Coughing, choking them down.

A thickness, heaviness, building up in his throat.

His chest.

His gut.

A drop of gluey warm.

Another drop.

Another drop.

Into the mountain.

Tears of molten sugar.

Tears of molten fat and salt.

He pauses, sadly.

Realizes, this is probably delicious.

But he cannot taste it.

He can only feel the weight of it.

Yes, he can only feel the ever-growing weight of it.
The weight of it becoming waste inside of him.

—

She lies, looking up at the glowing plastic constellations, after Marianne Lee's drifted off into some kind of sleep, into some mysterious dream life that does not appear to trouble her at all, at least not anywhere that she can see.

These made-up shapes. These made-up stories. Made-up tales made into histories. Made-up into the mapping of the sky. Made-up into the mapping of the made-up sky that makes her bedroom ceiling. Maybe she should sleep, now. Maybe she should shut her eyes.

How soft, the stillness that emerges from this movement.

How soft, the emptiness emerging from this fullness.

How soft, the churning acid froth.

How soft, the rising bile.

How soft, the boil, the slow, slow, slow, slow burning of it all.

So, so softly radiating. *With the energy within things.*

So, so softly gleaming. *With the loss, the failure to be someone else.*

So, so softly pulsing. *With the fear of what's to come.*
The fear of what you are—
of what you have—
become already.

—

20 years later, he is dead.
Well, he is living-dead.
Where he lives does not matter.
Whether he has moved, or stayed.
What he dreams does not matter.
What he does—most of all—does not matter
because he is not there, thinking, living, doing
anything.

—

20 years later, she is married to a woman.

No, it isn't Marianne Lee.

No, she is not happy.

Knows she is not happy.

She is what her wife—her partner—calls *content*, the thing her partner says replaces passion, what her partner says burns now, in place of fire.

Burning drive. A drive to keep the bits together. Drive to to keep the bits from burning. Sexless nights. Watching TV. Wineglasses in the dark. Falling asleep together on the couch. *Content*. She hates the way her partner gives a fucking name to this.

Some nights, she thinks about that night with Marianne Lee. And she feels regret.

Feels angry, stupid, for feeling regret.

After all, now she has a real life.

A wife who loves her.

Loves her for herself.

Loves being with her.

Loves her for who—what—she really is.

—

And so, it passes.
Finally.
The fires burn their way through August.
As they always do.
As everybody said they would.
The rain comes.
Smoke begins to fade, replaced by fog.
A shimmer-hover over brilliant yellow-gold.
Burnt-orange.
Deep-red leaves.
People emerge, now, from their boxes. For their weekend hikes. Their autumn festivals. The smells of cinnamon, roast pumpkin, cider spice. You are excited—as a matter of fact—because you are getting ready to go out—yes—to meet somebody out there.

You fill a hot bath. It is cool enough, at long last, to enjoy these sorts of things. A hot bath. Sinking down into the warmth. Submerging. Steam fogs up the mirror. Steam fills up the room and fills your mind. You rub the soap foam in-between your hands. You slick your legs. You point your toes to shave them—as you've seen beautiful women do, in films, in ads, in images you think of, as you do this—as you run the razor, slowly, from your ankle, up the middle of your calf muscle, the apex of your knee, the base of your thigh, and—Oh! Oh! You feel a sharp pierce. Feel the slitting of your skin. The rush of air. The infiltration of the air into your skin. You stare down at the space, the unmarked, soon-to-be-marked space, there, in your skin. You stare at it and wait, and wait, and wait, and wait, and wait, and wait, and wait, and wait, and wait, and wait, and wait, and wait, and wait, knowing the blood is going to come—soon—where is it, where is it, why hasn't it, why doesn't it, isn't it going to, it is, it will, won't it, doesn't it have to, yes, surely it has to, surely you did something, you felt something, yes, you know that you felt something, you felt something, yes, you know you felt it, yes, and it was real, wasn't it?

MEGHAN LAMB is the author of COWARD, *Failure to Thrive* (Apocalypse Party, 2021), *All of Your Most Private Places* (Spork Press, 2020), and *Silk Flowers* (Birds of Lace, 2017). She served as the Philip Roth Writer-in-Residence at Bucknell University in 2018, and has led creative workshops at the University of Chicago, Eötvös Loránd University, Interlochen Center for the Arts, and Washington University in St. Louis. Her work has appeared in *Quarterly West, DIAGRAM, Redivider*, and *Passages North*, among other publications. She currently serves as the nonfiction editor of *Nat. Brut*, a Whiting Award-winning journal of art and literature dedicated to advancing inclusivity in all creative fields.

Printed in the USA
CPSIA information can be obtained
at www.ICGtesting.com
LVHW031253150324
774517LV00049B/2615